Oi, CAVEBOY!

To my favourite daughter, Bridie,
who can be anything she wants to be

Bloomsbury Publishing, London, Berlin and New York

First published in Great Britain in April 2010 by Bloomsbury Publishing Plc
36 Soho Square, London W1D 3QY

A CIP catalogue record of this book is available from the British Library

ISBN 978 1 4088 0334 9

FSC
Mixed Sources
Product group from well-managed
forests and other controlled sources

Cert no. SGS - COC - 2061
www.fsc.org
© 1996 Forest Stewardship Council

Typeset by Dorchester Typesetting Group Ltd
Printed in Great Britain by Clays Ltd, St Ives Plc

3 5 7 9 10 8 6 4

www.bloomsbury.com

Oi, CAVEBOY!

ALAN MACDONALD

Illustrations by Mark Beech

BLOOMSBURY

LONDON BERLIN NEW YORK

Contents

Long, long ago...

Really ages ago. The world was a wild and barren place. There were no houses or shops, no schools or teachers, no cars, flushing toilets or peanut-butter sandwiches. So many things didn't exist that to write them all down would fill every page of this book and leave no room for the story.

If you want to imagine how the world was, imagine an endless landscape of mountains, forests, rocks and stones. In fact, stones lay everywhere, because this was . . .

1

THE STONE AGE

In the forests lived savage beasts — bears, snaggle-toothed tigers and woolly mammoths, which looked like elephants badly in need of a haircut. People generally avoided the forests. They lived together in tribes because it was safer that way and easier on the cooking. One such tribe was the Urks.

The Urks were a warlike race with bushy beards and hairy legs — especially some of the women. Their clothes were made of animal skins and they lived in caves high on a hill overlooking the Valley of Urk and the river winding through it. In one of these caves lived a boy called Iggy. He wasn't the tallest or the hairiest in his tribe, but what he did have was imagination, and this got him into a whole heap of trouble. That of course is another story ... Luckily it's the story that's about to begin ...

Chapter 1
No Lumps

Iggy woke to find his dad trying to light a fire —
a task that involved a few sticks, some dry
grass, two flints and a lot of cursing.

'Dung and blood!' he muttered under his
breath.

'Dad?' said Iggy, emerging from the shadows of
their cave.

'Not now, boy,' snapped Dad irritably. 'I'm
busy.'

For a while the only noise was Iggy trying not

to bother his dad, which sounded like silence with occasional sighing. Then . . .

'Dad, look at this.'

'FOR URK'S SAKE!' groaned Dad. 'How can I make a fire with you yammering in my ear?'

'Sorry, but look what I found.'

Dad turned his head. 'Uhh. A stone.'

'Yes, but it's flat. Look, no lumps.' Iggy ran his hand over the stone, which was long and smooth and roughly the shape of a squished cowpat.

'What about her?' said Dad.

'I just thought it might be useful.'

'Uhh,' grunted Dad, and went back to striking the flints together. He was in a bad mood. Lately he was often in a bad mood. It was the cold and damp and sleeping on a hard cave floor and never getting any peace and quiet.

Iggy squatted down beside him.

'Dad? You know the river? Where does it go?'

'Go?'

'Yes.'

'Don't go anywhere, her's a river. Pass us them sticks, boy.'

'But it must go somewhere.'

'Why?'

'Well, I was watching it yesterday and it moves. It sort of wibbles along.'

'Wibbles? Talk sense!'

'I mean it runs — it runs down the valley. But where's it go then?'

Dad pulled at his beard. He'd never given the river any thought. It was just there. Cold and wet – except in winter when it was cold and frozen.

'Dunged if I know,' he said.

Where did the boy get these ideas? Rivers that go somewhere. Stones with no bumps. Why couldn't he stick to things that mattered? Like fires – fires kept you warm and someone had to make them. He went back to striking the two flints together. A spark flew and caught the dry grass. He crouched over it, shielding it from the wind.

Iggy turned his attention back to the flat stone, wondering what he could do with it. He set it down and prodded it with his foot. It skittered

forward like a pebble on ice. He put his head on one side the way he did when he was having an idea.

Dad meanwhile went on muttering and feeding the tiny flames with twigs and grass. A wisp of grey smoke curled upwards. Iggy placed one foot on the big flat stone and pushed gently. Sure enough it slid forward a little. *What if I try both feet?* he thought. He shoved off hard in the dirt and the next moment shot forward at the speed of a jet-propelled boomerang.

'Arrgggggh!' yelled Dad, which isn't really a word but is the kind of thing you shout when you're bowled over by a boy on a runaway stone.

Iggy hit the cave wall, bounced off and landed

with a bump. He rubbed his elbow.

'Whoa! Deadly!' he said.

Dad sat up with grass in his hair.

'You great noggerhead! Look what you done!'

Iggy saw the fire had gone out. Actually it had more than gone out – it looked like a rhinoceros had sat on it.

'Sorry, I couldn't stop,' he said.

'It took us hours to get that lit!'

'But, Dad, I scudded on the stone! Did you see me?'

'See you?' said Dad. 'You dung near run me over!'

'Sorry,' said Iggy. 'I just thought it could be useful.'

'You think too much,' said Dad. 'When I were your age I were out throwing rocks, chasing lizards. I didn't waste time flamin' thinking.'

Iggy said nothing. He had heard this a million times.

'If you want to do something useful, sharpen them flints,' said Dad.

Lately Dad had been teaching him how to make a hunting axe. But it was dull, slow work, chipping away at a lump of flint, and his attempts looked more like knobbly potatoes than axe-blades. He picked up the stone and dusted it off. Maybe he would show it to Hubba later.

Mum arrived at the cave, carrying a bundle of animal skins.

'Hasn't you got that fire going yet?' she grumbled.

'Her went out,' muttered Dad.

'Why did you let her go out, you big mumpet!'

'I didn't *let* her,' said Dad. 'Her went. Twigs must be damp.'

He glanced over at Iggy, who shot him a grateful look. Dad in a temper was bad enough, but Mum was much worse. Iggy had seen her pick a grown man up by the ears and bash him against the roof of the cave.

'Look at them skins!' she was saying. 'I just got the blood off 'em and now they're soggy as a frog. Hasn't I told you to bring 'em in?'

'Oh,' said Iggy. 'I forgot.'

'Forgot. You always forgot,' grunted Mum. 'Daydreaming as usual.' She spread the skins on a rock and looked at Dad expectantly. 'Well? Has you talked to him then?'

'Not yet,' said Dad. 'I been busy.'

'Talked to me about what?' asked Iggy.

Mum and Dad exchanged looks.

'Sit you down, boy,' said Dad. 'And for once try to listen without bugging in all the time.'

Iggy sat down. Whatever his parents wanted to talk about, it was obviously serious.

Dad took a deep breath. 'You know why you never been hunting?'

Iggy nodded. 'I'm not old enough yet.'

'Exactly. But your ma and me, we been talking

and, well, maybe it's time.'

Iggy leapt to his feet. 'I CAN GO HUNTING?'

'Let me finish,' said Dad. 'First you got to prove you're ready.'

'I am ready,' said Iggy.

'Well, that's what we're disgusting,' said Dad. 'You know what tomorrow is, don't you?'

Iggy shook his head.

'The Feast of Urks,' said Mum, nodding her head slowly.

Iggy's heart jumped a beat. The Feast of Urks took place on the night of the full moon, when the tribe gathered to see boys become Sons of Urk. Once you were a Son of Urk you could call yourself a warrior and join the older men on hunting expeditions. Iggy had often watched his dad set off for the forest, wishing he could go along. Now his time had finally come – although he had a funny feeling it wasn't that simple.

'What will I have to do?' he asked.

'Nothing much,' said Dad, with a quick glance at Mum. 'All you do is go up when Uncle Ham calls your name.'

(Uncle Ham was High Chief, though most people called him Hammerhead or just Chief.)

'And that's all?' asked Iggy.

Dad nodded. 'All there is to it – apart from the Testing.'

'The Testing?'

Mum nodded. 'You can't be a Son of Urk unless you pass the Testing.'

'But how? How do I pass?'

'The usual way,' said Dad. 'By killing a snake.'

'A SNAKE?' Iggy gulped. 'Couldn't I kill a beetle or something?'

'No,' said Mum. 'Got to be a snake.'

She was smiling as if nothing could be simpler.

'Don't go getting in a muck sweat,' said Dad. 'No one's asking you to kill 'em with your bare hands. Look, I made you something.'

Dad reached under a skin and brought out something heavy. It was a hunting axe with a new flint blade bound at the top.

'Um . . . thanks,' said Iggy.

Chapter 2
Snake Handling for Beginners

'**B**rilliant!' declared Hubba. 'I'm going too. So we'll both be taking the Testing! That's so brilliant it's almost . . .'

'Brilliant?' said Iggy.

'Yes!'

They had been trying out the flat stone, taking it in turns to slide down the steep muddy slope. Mostly they fell off or hit a bump and fell off.

'Better'n walking,' said Hubba. 'We could go everywhere with this.'

'As long as everywhere was downhill,' agreed Iggy.

'So what you gonna call her, like?'

'Don't know. A flat-stone, maybe,' said Iggy.

Hubba picked up the stone and brushed off the dirt, giving it some thought. 'Scootboard,' he said.

'Why?'

'Dunno. Just sounds good.'

Iggy tried out the word a few times. It did sort of sound right.

'All right. Scootboard it is,' he agreed.

Hubba grinned, pleased with himself. Words weren't usually his strong point.

They sat down side by side, looking out over the misty grey valley.

'Maybe it still needs something else,' said Iggy. 'I could fix something underneath.'

Hubba nodded. 'Like rocks, you mean?'

'No.'

'Grass then?'

'No! Something to make it run faster.'

'Rabbits,' said Hubba.

Iggy gave him a look. He laid the scootboard aside, deciding to work on it later. Right now there were other things to worry about, like tonight's feast. At least he had the comfort of knowing Hubba would be there and had to pass the Testing too.

'You're not worried, are you?' he asked.

'Me? No!' scoffed Hubba.

'Nor me,' said Iggy gloomily.

'Just think,' said Hubba. 'Come tomorrow we can go hunting like proper, you know . . .'

'. . . Hunters,' said Iggy. He leaned forward, resting his chin on his arms. 'Snakes though. Why's it have to be snakes?'

'That's all right. I know a lot about snakes,' said Hubba.

'Do you?' Iggy looked at him in surprise.

Hubba nodded, leaning in closer. 'For one thing, they got no legs.'

'Right. So you reckon you can kill one?'

'Easy. They won't be running off.'

'Hubba,' said Iggy, 'have you ever seen a snake?'

'Hundreds of times. Seen one under a rock once. Pink her was, a weeny, wiggly little beast.'

'You mean a worm?'

'Oh.'

'Snakes are usually bigger,' said Iggy. 'A lot bigger. With fangs.'

'Umm,' said Hubba, frowning. 'So you can't just squish 'em with your foot?'

'Not unless you want to get bitten.'

Hubba thought this over while scratching his belly. Killing a snake was obviously going to be much tougher than he'd realised.

Footsteps approached and a shadow fell over them.

Iggy groaned. It was Snark — the last person in the world he wanted to see. Snark was big for his age. He had a blunt, scowling face that reminded Iggy of a woolly rhino, though obviously less intelligent. He was the junior tribal champion at boulder ball and headbanger, but his favourite sport was torturing Iggy. Iggy didn't know why Snark picked on him in particular.

'We're busy,' said Iggy.

'That so?' Snark wiped his mouth. 'Thought you'd be practising for tonight. My dad says it's just you, me and Dum-Dum.'

'Don't call him that,' said Iggy.

'Why? Gonna sit on me, Dum-Dum? Oooh, I'm scared!'

Hubba studied the ground. He knew from bitter experience that getting into a fight with Snark would only end in humiliation. It was best to keep your mouth shut and hope he would go away.

'So? Nervous?' asked Snark.

Iggy shrugged, trying to look unconcerned. 'They're only snakes. Shouldn't be too hard.'

'Ah well, depends on the snake, like,' said Snark, showing his small yellow teeth. 'Grass snakes – them's harmless, wouldn't bite a fly. But there's other kinds. Ever seen a swamp snake?'

Iggy shook his head.

'Proper huge they are. Especially the black-bellied swamp snake – that's a beast! But the best part's how they kill you.'

'I'm
not that
interested,'
said Iggy, whose palms were
starting to sweat.

'A swamp snake doesn't bite
– that'd be over too quick, see?'
said Snark. 'No, her wraps her
coils around you – round your
legs, round your belly, slithering
all over you. Then, when you can't
escape, her starts to *squeeze*. Tighter
and tighter, till you can't hardly breathe till
your eyes pop out and your face
turns blue.'

Iggy had gone pale. 'I'm sure they won't be giving us swamp snakes,' he said.

'Cut off her head, that's what I'd do,' said Snark. 'Course, you got to be quick with an axe.'

He drew out a wicked-looking axe from his belt and twirled it expertly, before tossing it high. The axe hummed as it spun in the air, reaching the top of its arc before plunging towards them. Without even glancing up, Snark reached out a hand and caught it neatly by the handle. He grinned and held out the axe to Iggy.

'You have a go.'

'No, thanks.'

'Go on! Don't be a yellow-belly!'

'Show him, Iggy,' said Hubba.

Iggy swallowed hard and grasped the rough wooden handle. He had always been nervous around axes. His dad said you should never play with them. He gathered himself before hurling the axe high, higher in fact than he'd intended. For a moment he lost sight of it in the sunlight, then he saw it plummeting towards him like a hawk out of the sky.

THUNK!

It bit the ground, though Iggy didn't see where it landed since he was curled in a ball with his eyes closed.

Snark laughed and picked up his axe, wiping the mud off the blade.

'Good luck tonight,' he said. 'Looks like you're gonna need it. Hur hur!'

They watched him swagger off up the hill, laughing to himself and shaking his head.

'He's just trying to scare us,' said Iggy.

Hubba nodded.

'Black-bellied swamp snake! I bet he made that up. Anyway, they'll only be giving us grass snakes.'

'You think?' said Hubba.

'Definitely,' nodded Iggy, sounding more confident than he felt. All the same, he didn't want to leave anything to chance. If he was going to kill a snake in front of the whole tribe, he would need something better than a flint-head axe. With an axe you would need to get close enough to launch an attack. Miss, and the snake would sink her fangs into your arm — or some other tender part of you. Then if it was poisonous, you would start to sweat and feel dizzy, which, come to think of it, was how he was feeling right now. Knowing that Snark was a candidate for the Testing only made matters worse. Iggy stooped to pick up a piece of bone from the dust. 'There must be some other way,' he said.

'What?' said Hubba.

'To kill a snake.'

'Oh. You could always use a spear.'

Iggy shook his head. Spear throwing wasn't his strong point. He doubted he could hit a tree, let alone a snake that wouldn't keep still. He examined the bone he had found. It was the curved jawbone of some animal. Iggy turned it over in his hand, thinking.

Chapter 3
The Feast of Urks

Iggy fiddled with the piece of bone while he waited to be called. The feast had begun at sunset and had now been going for three hours. Darkness had closed in and clouds were racing across the full moon. For Iggy it had been an agony of waiting. He could see smoke billowing into the sky and smell the delicious aroma of roasting meat. Every now and then someone would strike up the Urk war cry with the drums and a hundred other voices would join in.

Ugga ugga oogie!
Urk! Urk! Urk!
Ging gang goolie !
Urk! Urk ! Urk!

No one was entirely sure what this meant, but the Urks had been bellowing it for generations. Iggy glanced at Hubba, who was pacing up and down, talking to himself. Snark sat alone on a rock, stifling a yawn as if killing snakes was something he could do in his sleep.

Footsteps approached, and Iggy rose to his

feet. It was Dad.

'Ready?' he said.

Iggy nodded.

'Them're waiting. Got your axe?'

'Yes.'

'Don't forget, aim for the head,' Dad whispered. 'That's the end with the eyes and teeth.'

'I know, Dad.'

'And don't let 'em know you're scared. Snakes can smell your fear. Or is that wolves? I never can remember. Anyhow . . . what's that?'

Dad pointed to the jawbone Iggy was fiddling with. A piece of lizard gut hung loose, stretched between the two ends.

'It's nothing,' said Iggy.

Hubba stuck his head between them. 'It's a clutterpult!' he said. 'Iggy made her. It's deadly.'

Dad frowned. It didn't look deadly to him. It looked like a scraggy old bit of bone.

Just then they were interrupted by a deafening blast on a mammoth horn.

'The Chief,' said Dad. 'Better go.' He looked at Iggy. 'For Urk's sake, boy, don't try anything daft.'

Iggy stuffed the catapult inside his furs. To tell the truth, he wasn't at all sure this was going to work. Earlier he had practised with the catapult, using a large boulder as a target. He'd scored two out of ten – and one of those was a lucky rebound. Still, it was better than his axe skills.

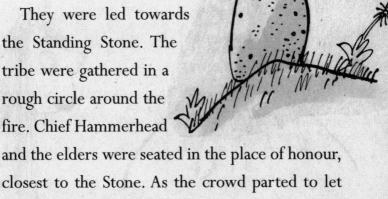

They were led towards
the Standing Stone. The
tribe were gathered in a
rough circle around the
fire. Chief Hammerhead
and the elders were seated in the place of honour,
closest to the Stone. As the crowd parted to let
the three boys through, Iggy felt eyes measuring
him, which didn't take long as there wasn't much
to measure.

Chief Hammerhead was wearing his ceremonial
necklace, the one made of whalebones. No one
would have guessed that the Chief and Iggy's
Dad were brothers. With his tangled red hair
Hammerhead looked like he'd been left out in the

rain to go rusty. The Urks regarded hairiness as a sign of manliness, which was one reason why the Chief was held in great respect. His chest was so hairy you could have made a dozen rugs from it. From the back he looked like a bear. Sitting next to the Chief was his daughter, Umily. Iggy tried not to look at her in case he did that gormless staring-with-his-mouth-open thing. He wished his hands would stop shaking.

The drumming died away and a hush fell over the gathering.

Hammerhead raised his voice. 'Friends, brothers, Men of Urk . . .' A low growl came from the back rows. 'And Women of Urk,' he added quickly. 'Tonight we has gathered to welcome three young warriors into the tribe. They wish to become Sons of Urk!'

'Urk! Urk! Urk!' chanted the crowd.

The Chief turned to the three candidates before him.

'This is a night for courage, honour and, most

of all . . . for KILLING SNAKES!'

The crowd roared their approval. It was always a pleasure seeing the younger members of the tribe, but it was even better watching a snake split in half.

Iggy tried not to think about the ordeal ahead. He studied the faces behind Hammerhead but found his eyes kept coming back to his cousin Umily. Unlike most Urks, her hair was fair and looked as if it might even have been washed. Iggy thought it shone like sunbeams on a lake or like the skin of a lizard — although maybe he wouldn't tell her that. He tried to concentrate on the ceremony. Snark and Hubba were being presented to the Chief. He was next. He reminded himself not to call him Uncle Ham.

'Iggy!' boomed Hammerhead, crushing him in his arms. He looked him up and down.

'Ah well, plenty of time to grow, eh?' he said, bellowing as if Iggy was deaf. 'So you want to be a Son of Urk?'

Iggy nodded.

'You swear to be a true Urk, to honour the tribe and serve your Chief?'

'I swear,' said Iggy.

'Splendid!' beamed Hammerhead. 'That's the dull bit over – let's get you in that snake pit, eh?'

Snake pit? Iggy's stomach lurched. His dad hadn't mentioned anything about a snake pit! They were led over to a large muddy hole lit by a circle of flaming torches. It was as deep as a grave, which didn't strike Iggy as a cheering thought. At least it wasn't filled with a sea of writhing snakes. Iggy wondered when they were going to appear. He soon found out as a man stepped into the fire-light carrying a bulging sack. It was Snark's father, Borg, chief elder of the tribe. He lifted the sack high above his head for the crowd to see.

'Ooooh!' they gasped.

The sack was jumping and rippling as if it was alive. Iggy felt he might be sick.

At a signal from Hammerhead, the drumming began again. The crowd pressed in to get a better view, forcing Iggy closer to the edge of the pit. He prayed that he wouldn't have to go first, but he needn't have worried: Snark always went first.

Snark jumped down and landed in the pit with his long-handled axe at the ready. All eyes turned to Borg as he loosened the neck of the sack and fished inside with a forked stick. He pulled out a hissing snake, which thrashed from side to side. It wasn't a very big snake. If Iggy hadn't known

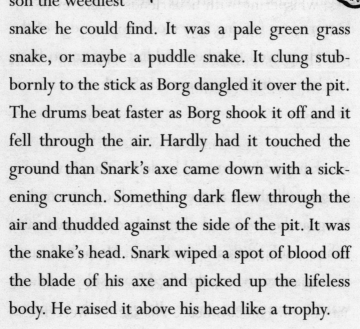

better, he would
have said Borg
had chosen his
son the weediest
snake he could find. It was a pale green grass
snake, or maybe a puddle snake. It clung stub-
bornly to the stick as Borg dangled it over the pit.
The drums beat faster as Borg shook it off and it
fell through the air. Hardly had it touched the
ground than Snark's axe came down with a sick-
ening crunch. Something dark flew through the
air and thudded against the side of the pit. It was
the snake's head. Snark wiped a spot of blood off
the blade of his axe and picked up the lifeless
body. He raised it above his head like a trophy.

'URK! URK ! URK!
URK! URK! URK!'

chanted the crowd. Iggy noticed Umily smiling
and whispering with her friends. Snark evidently
had a lot of admirers.

'Three seconds,' muttered Hubba. 'Pretty
deadly, you got to admit.'

Iggy rolled his eyes. 'Oh come on, it was a
tiddler! My gran could have killed it!'

Hubba was up next. His opponent was a
mud-coloured rock snake which coiled itself
sleepily round the stick and didn't want to let
go. When Borg finally shook it loose, it almost
landed on Hubba's head. His tactics were messy

but effective. He jumped around hacking and swiping like a madman. By the end there was blood and guts everywhere and very little left of the snake. Hubba was helped out of the pit, beaming triumphantly as the crowd cheered.

Finally it was Iggy's turn. He tried to ignore the way his heart was beating faster than the drums. At least the snakes he'd seen so far weren't big or poisonous. He edged closer to the pit and peered in. The next moment someone shoved him in the back and he fell, landing flat on his face. Iggy heard laughter that sounded suspiciously like Snark.

By the time he was on his feet Borg was already fishing the next snake out of the sack. The front row gasped and took a step back. Iggy stared in horror. The snake was a monster. It looked like it ate scorpions for breakfast. What's more, it didn't seem too pleased to be dragged out of a sack and dangled over a muddy hole by a stick.

'Wait!' cried Hubba. 'That's a . . .'

But Borg paid no attention at all and the snake landed in the pit with a heavy thump. Iggy leapt back. The snake raised its head and its pink tongue flickered out.

'HISSSSSSSSSSSSSSSSSSSS!'

'Iggy! Don't move!' cried Hubba. 'I don't think her's a grass snake.'

Iggy swallowed hard. 'I guessed that,' he murmured.

'Isn't it one of them . . .' Hubba tried to remember. 'Oh . . . you know . . .'

'A black-bellied swamp snake?' It was Snark who had spoken. He crouched at the edge of the pit, peering into it.

'Funny, you don't see 'em too often,' he said. 'Except in swamps, of course. Wonder how her got in the sack?'

Iggy thought he saw a sly look pass between Snark and his father. Maybe they had planned this all along.

'Is it . . . . poisonous?' he breathed.

'Probably,' said Snark. 'Maybe you should ask her.'

The snake was swaying from side to side in a hypnotic dance, its yellow eyes locked on Iggy.

'Don't just stand there! Use your axe, boy!' cried Dad.

Iggy would have gladly used his axe, but the moment he made any sudden movement the snake would strike, sinking its fangs into his arm

– or somewhere more painful. Instead he slowly reached his hand into his furs and brought out the catapult. His mouth turned dry. He had forgotten the one thing he needed: ammunition! Earlier he had collected a stock of pebbles, but he'd used them all up in target practice. He was a sitting duck – and pretty soon he would be a dead duck.

Glancing down, he spotted a couple of small stones lying in the mud. The problem was they were close to the snake. Very, very slowly, Iggy stooped and reached out a hand, keeping his eyes on his enemy. He could hear the fire crackling and the crowd holding their breath. Hubba watched through a crack in his fingers. Iggy's dad was holding his head in his hands. What on Urk was the boy playing at?

Iggy's fingers closed over the stones. Feverishly he fitted one to his catapult. The swamp snake swayed as he took aim at the head.

FTUUUUNKKKKK!

The stone belly-flopped in the mud, falling hopelessly short. Startled, the snake darted its head forward inches from Iggy's face.

'HISSSSSSSSSSSS!'

Iggy fumbled with the catapult, trying to fit the second pebble. The snake's jaws were open wide, showing its tiny fangs. Iggy drew the sling back to breaking point and let fly.

FTAAAAANNNG!

This time he lost his footing and stumbled backwards in the mud. When he opened his eyes he could see rows of faces looking down at him from above. Had he missed? Was he bitten? A loud roaring filled his ears.

'URK! URK! URK!
URK! URK! URK!'

Iggy propped himself on his elbows. The snake was lying dead, slumped on one side with eyes closed and fangs still bared.

'URK! URK! URK!'

He had done it. He'd actually killed a snake, and not some puny little grass snake but a giant black-bellied swamp snake. He had proved himself a true Son of Urk. Giddy with triumph, Iggy picked up the snake by the tail, and swung it round his head a few times before letting it go.

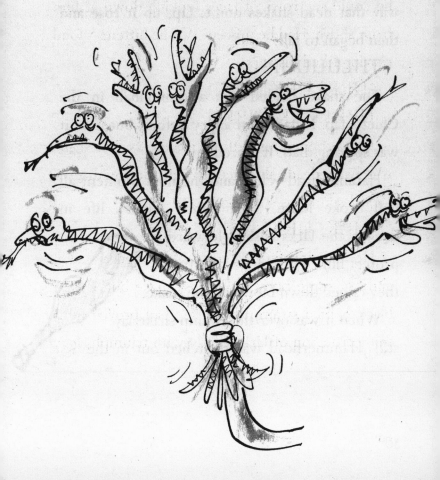

The swamp snake soared out of the pit and high into the sky. It snapped open its eyes in exactly the way that dead snakes don't. Up, up it rose and then began to fall.

THLUUUUP!

The snake landed like a cannonball in the Chief's lap. It had been angry before, but now it was spitting mad. It reared up.

Hammerhead yelled and the next moment all hell broke loose. Seeing their Chief's life in danger, the Urks rushed forward to protect him. With clubs and sticks they rained down blows on the snake.

When it was over the swamp snake lay still. Hammerhead was stretched out in the dust, moaning faintly.

There was a long, awkward silence.

Followed by an even longer one.

'Chief?' said Borg, who had been the first to rush to Hammerhead's rescue, swinging a heavy club. 'Chief? Are you all right? Say something.'

'Urrrhhhh!' said Hammerhead, who was covered in lumps and bruises.

Borg shook his head gravely. He beckoned to some of the men, who came forward and carried their leader back to his cave. (It took six of them.) Shortly after, the rest of the tribe began to melt away, shaking their heads sadly and talking in low voices — until no one was left at all.

Almost no one.

'HELLO?' cried Iggy from the bottom of the
pit. 'Can somebody help me out of here?'

Chapter 4
The Elders
Speak

The next day didn't bring good news. Hammerhead had fallen into a dangerous fever since the snake attack. Most people said he had been bitten, but some blamed evil spirits, while others thought it might have something to do with being beaten by heavy clubs. Either way, the Urks went about their business with long faces and heavy hearts. Hammerhead had been

Chief for as long as anyone could remember, and a future without him was unthinkable. Even those who tried to think the unthinkable found it was like staring into a dark bottomless pit with their eyes closed.

Gaga the Wise took charge of nursing the Chief back to health. Of all the tribal elders, he was the oldest and wisest. People claimed he was over two hundred years old, although admittedly most of them had trouble counting up to five. Gaga spent long hours in the Chief's cave, mixing potions of ragweed, nettles, toad's blood and bat droppings. Yet Hammerhead only grew worse and sometimes threw up on the floor.

Iggy meanwhile had spent a cold, miserable

night in the snake pit. When it was light his parents and Hubba managed to sneak along to see if he was all right. According to Hubba, most of the tribe blamed Iggy for the accident. The elders had called a meeting for that evening and he would be summoned to appear.

Later that night the elders gathered in a circle around the Standing Stone. There were six of them in all, counting Borg and Gaga the Wise. Iggy thought they looked like ancient sea turtles

who had crawled out of their shells. He was glad to be free of the snake pit, but had no idea what lay ahead of him now.

In the absence of Hammerhead, Borg had decided to take charge. He was a small, bald man with staring eyes and a temper as short as his legs. He waited impatiently for the other elders to stop whispering and shuffling their feet.

'So. We all know why we has met?'

The elders nodded their grey heads, smiling vaguely.

'Is it the Chief's birthday?' asked one.

Borg raised his eyes heavenwards. Meetings of the elders always seemed to go like this – the longest had lasted six weeks.

'Let's be clear,' he said. 'We has called this meeting to punish the traitor.'

Iggy looked around, wondering who the traitor could be.

'Step forward, boy,' ordered Borg.

Iggy stepped into the circle, feeling dizzy and light-headed. He'd had nothing to eat since a handful of snails for breakfast.

'There's been some mistake . . .' he began.

'Silence when you speak to the elders!' roared Borg.

'Sorry,' said Iggy.

The elder called Sedric was pointing at him. 'Who is he?'

'The boy, Sedric,' whispered his neighbour.

'Is it *his* birthday?'

Borg silenced them with a furious look. He turned to Iggy. 'Answer, boy. Does you deny trying to murder the Chief?'

'No . . . I mean, yes, it was an accident!' stammered Iggy.

Borg gave a dry laugh. 'Hah! You expect us to believe that?'

'It's true! I thought the snake was dead.'

'Then why did you throw her at the Chief?'

'I wasn't aiming at him!' said Iggy. 'I just got carried away. It was an accident!'

'So you keeps saying,' said Borg grimly. He turned to the circle of elders. 'Does anyone here wish to speak for the boy?'

Iggy waited hopefully. None of the elders spoke or got to their feet. Either they hadn't understood the question or they were too frightened of Borg to say a word. Gaga the Wise had his eyes closed and his hands clasped in his lap. He looked like he'd nodded off to sleep. Iggy wondered where his mum and dad could be.

'Then shall us deal with the question of punishment?' said Borg, hurrying them on.

Iggy thought he must have misheard.

'But I haven't –'

'SILENCE!' roared Borg.

'But –'

'Hold your tongue! For the last time, does anyone wish to question the boy?'

A hand went up. It belonged to Sedric.

'What is your favourite colour?' he asked.

Iggy groaned. He'd get more sense from a mushroom.

Borg had lost patience and was already moving on. 'We has heard enough,' he said. 'I ask the elders to pass judgement. You saw it happen with your own eyes. Were this just an accident? Or were it something else? A cold-blooded plot to murder our beloved Chief.'

'Who?' asked Sedric, cupping his ear.

'The Chief.'

'I thought he weren't coming.'

'He's not. He were bitten by a snake!'

'Great Urk! Has anyone told him?'

'WILL YOU SHUT UP?' roared Borg, thudding his axe into the ground, which had the desired effect of getting everyone's attention.

'As I were saying, the law of the tribe is clear. If any Urk shall strike his Chief, he must be cast out. Banished once and for all.'

'*Banished?*' Iggy gasped. He had expected a severe telling-off, but banished? How would he survive outside of the tribe, without food or shelter?

Borg was passing among the elders, handing each of them a small grey pebble. He came to a halt in the middle of the circle and spoke in a loud, ringing voice.

'Elders of Urk, give your judgement. If you

find the boy guilty of murder, cast your stone into the circle.'

The wind had dropped. It had suddenly grown so quiet you could have heard a worm counting its legs. Or a squirrel thinking of acorns. Or a . . . Anyway, it was very, very quiet.

Iggy knew his fate rested on the elders and the six grey pebbles in their hands. If more than three stones were cast into the circle, he was doomed.

Borg opened his hand. The first stone rolled in the dust. He glared impatiently at the other elders and a second pebble thudded into the circle.

'Wait!'

Iggy looked up and saw Hubba pushing through the crowd. Behind him came Mum and Dad, looking anxious and out of breath.

'For Urk's sake, stop this!' cried Dad. 'The boy made a mistake. He meant no harm!'

'Too late,' snapped Borg. 'You are not part of this council. The elders has reached a judgement.'

'Not quite,' said a voice. Every head turned to see who had spoken. It was Gaga the Wise, who up till now Iggy had assumed was asleep.

'You speak of "murder", Borg,' he said. 'But tell me – who is dead?'

Borg scowled at him furiously. 'You said yourself . . .'

'I said the Chief had a fever. He is sick, very sick. But the gods may grant he recovers. Surely that's what all of us hope?'

'Well . . . of course,' stammered Borg, turning red for some reason.

Gaga laced his pale fingers, resting them in his lap. He glanced at the dark clouds drifting across the sky. 'Allow me to make a suggestion,' he said. 'In the Farlands to the north grows a plant called the Purple Stankwort. Some of you may have heard of it.'

There was silence.

'The plant's juice is a powerful medicine,' Gaga

continued. 'I'm told it can cure almost anything. Perhaps even snakebites.'

Borg folded his arms. 'All well and good. But what dung fool would risk his neck going to the Farlands?'

Gaga smiled pleasantly. 'Perhaps a fool who wishes to make amends.'

Iggy blinked. Why was everyone staring in his direction?

Chapter 5
Farewell to Urk

Early next morning Iggy gathered the few things he needed for the long journey ahead.

He had never been to the Farlands. In fact, he'd never been out of the Valley of Urk. Part of him was looking forward to discovering the wide world beyond the river, but he might have felt better if Mum and Dad weren't acting as if they would never see him again.

His mum hugged him for the third time that

morning and thumped him on the back. 'You promise to be careful now?'

'I promise,' sighed Iggy.

'Keep away from them forests and anything that could eat you.'

'I will,' said Iggy. 'Anyway, I've got my catapult.'

'Flaming Urk!' muttered Dad.

Mum ruffled Iggy's hair and sniffed.

'I'll be fine, Mum,' said Iggy. 'In a few days' time I'll be back.'

'Course you will,' sniffed Mum, wiping her eyes. 'Don't mind me. It's just the smoke from the fire.'

Dad seemed to be having trouble with his eyes

too. 'You be careful, boy,' he said gruffly. 'It's not safe out there.'

'I know, Dad,' said Iggy. 'There are wolves and woolaphants.'

'Not just them. Worse things,' said Dad darkly. 'Come, there's something you should see.'

He led the way up the hill, along a track that Iggy didn't know. Eventually they reached a ledge high above the valley, where he pulled aside some brambles to reveal the mouth of a cave. Iggy thought he knew all the caves in the Valley of Urk, but he'd never entered this one. He wondered why his dad had never spoken of it before. Inside they followed the passage, which eventually opened out into a large shadowy cavern. Iggy stopped and stared. The walls were covered in strange paintings. There were pictures of wolves, deer and bison that looked so real that he didn't dare get too close. Dad walked past them all and stopped at another painting. It showed tiny ant-like men being chased by a race of giants armed with spears and clubs. Some of the ant-men lay on the ground in bright red pools of blood. One of them was running around without his head.

'Them were painted long ago, before my time,' said Dad.

'Who are they?' asked Iggy, tracing the outline of one of the giants.

'Nonecks,' said Dad. 'That's what we call 'em.'

'Nonecks?' Iggy had never heard the word before.

'They're a tribe in the Farlands. If you meet a Noneck, then you run, boy. Don't stop or smile or chat about the weather. Just run.'

'Why?' said Iggy.

'Because Nonecks are savages,' said Dad.

Iggy stared at the towering giants chasing the scared little men. 'But how will I know if they're Nonecks?'

'You'll know,' said Dad grimly. 'They're not

like us. Mind what I say — you run.'

Iggy nodded. Suddenly he wasn't looking forward to exploring the wide world beyond the river quite as much.

Dad thought for a moment and reached inside his furs. 'Here, take 'em,' he said.

Iggy looked down at the black sharp-edged stones.

'They're your flints. How will you make a fire?'

'Plenty more where them came from. You keep 'em, and mind you bring 'em back.' Dad pressed the flints into his hand and looked away, wiping his eyes even though there was no smoke.

'Go on now,' he said. 'There's someone waiting for you.'

Iggy hurried down the hillside, hoping it might be Umily. Perhaps she had come to thank him for risking his life to save her father. And when the time came to say goodbye, her pale blue eyes would fill with tears. She would hold his hand and say . . .

'There you are, you great swallop! I been waiting ages!'

It wasn't his beautiful cousin; it was Hubba.

'Oh,' said Iggy, trying to hide his disappointment. 'Come to see me off?'

Hubba grinned broadly. 'Nope.'

'To wish me luck then?'

'No point.'

'Why not?'

'Cos I'm coming with you.'

'Hubba, no! You can't!'

'Who says I can't?'

Iggy tried to argue but he was wasting his breath. Once Hubba had made up his mind he stuck to it and nothing would shift him. Besides, Iggy was secretly relieved. Adventures were all very well, but they were much better with two of you.

*

Soon Iggy and Hubba were heading down the valley, chatting happily as if it was just another morning and they were going to hunt for yumberries.

'Hubba,' said Iggy, 'have you ever wondered where the river goes?'

'Nope.'

'But where do you think?'

'Don't know.'

'It must go somewhere.'

'Never thought about it.'

'But if you had to take a guess?'

'Round the corner.'

'Then where?'

'Don't know.'

While this pointless discussion went on, two dark figures were watching from high above the valley.

'Heh heh heh!' Borg laughed his evil laugh, which was deeper and more evil than his everyday laugh.

'Hur hur hur!' sniggered his dim-witted son. 'Shall us throw a rock at them, Dad?'

'Don't be stupid, Snark.'

'Just a little rock. Shall us?'

'I said put it down!'

Snark dropped the rock with a sulky gesture.

'This is all working out even better than I planned,' said Borg.

'Is it?' said Snark.

'Any day now that bone-brain Hammerhead will be dead and the elders will name a new Chief. You know what that means?'

Snark looked blank.

'Think, boy. A new Chief, someone close to you.'

'Umily!' cried Snark.

'Not Umily, you bogtrotter! I mean me, Borg.

And once I'm Chief, no one will stand in my way. Heh heh heh!'

'Hur hur hur!' said Snark, watching the two boys wade across the river. 'But, Dad, what about Iggy?'

'What about him?'

'You said he were gonna be Chief one day. Being as Hammerhead's his uncle.'

'That, Snark, is why we put a swamp snake in the sack, remember?'

'Oh yeah, that were funny. Hur hur! Pity it didn't bite him though.'

'This way is better,' said Borg. 'Hammerhead dies and his runty little nephew gets sent to the Farlands. It's perfect!'

'Yes,' said Snark. 'Except for the Stinkweed.'

'What stinkweed?'

'You know, the flower that Gaga were talking about. What if Iggy finds her and brings her back? What if the Chief gets better?'

'What if? What if?' snapped Borg. 'What if I poke you in the eye?'

'Ow!'

Borg gave his son a withering look. Sometimes he wondered if he had the brain of a gnat. When Borg became Chief, Snark would be next in line, which was a worrying thought.

'Anyway,' he said, 'you think some scrubby old weed can save Hammerhead?'

'Dunno,' said Snark, rubbing his eye. 'It might.'

'Rubbish!' snapped Borg. 'Even if it exists, they'll never find it. Why do you think no one ever goes to the Farlands?'

'Cos they're too far?' said Snark.

'Because they never come back. That's the last we'll see of your two little friends. They're good as dead.'

Borg threw back his head and his evil laughter echoed across the valley.

HA! HA! HA! HA!

HA! HA! HA!

HA! HA!

Ha!

Chapter 6
Talking in Grunts

Iggy trudged uphill through a swirling grey fog. He felt they had been walking for ever – at least since the day before yesterday. They had waded through rivers, hurried though dark forests and toiled across moors where the wind was colder than a snowman's toes. Now they seemed to be entering a dismal land of marsh and bog. Bubbles flipped and flopped in pools of mud.

Hot steam spat into the air with a sound like a giant belching. Iggy shivered and waited for Hubba to catch up.

'Anything left to eat?' he asked.

Hubba reached into his furs and brought out a purple-stained hand.

'Two billyberries,' he said. 'They're a bit squished, but I been keeping 'em warm.'

'Thanks, but you have them,' said Iggy. He peered into the damp mist. He was beginning to wonder if they would ever reach the Farlands. Soon it would be evening and too dark to find their way.

'We should rest,' he said. 'You go and look for firewood.'

Hubba looked round. 'In them woods?'

'Woods are usually the best place.'

'Yes.' Hubba still hung back. 'Only what if I meet a wolf or a grizzler?'

'Here,' said Iggy. 'Take my catapult. And whistle – it'll scare them off.'

'Oh. Thanks.' Hubba set off for the trees, whistling the kind of tune that sends bears and wolves running for cover. Iggy meanwhile gathered some sticks and moss into a small pile and tried to get a spark to start the fire. The flints reminded him of home and he wished he was back in his own damp-smelling cave, listening to Mum grumbling over the supper. Footsteps approached.

'Something's coming!' he panted.

Iggy narrowed his eyes, peering into the mist. At first he thought Hubba had imagined it, but then he glimpsed a grey shape. Whatever it was, it was moving fast and coming their way. It walked on two legs, which meant it was either human or a bear showing off.

'Iggy,' said Hubba nervously, 'I think us should go back.'

'Stay calm . . . stay calm,' said Iggy.

'I am calm. You're hurting my arm!'

'He's probably friendly. Just act like you mean no harm.'

Hubba raised a hand and waved, though it

might have looked more friendly if he hadn't been holding a stick.

The stranger had reached the clearing. Like them he was dressed in furs, but no one would have mistaken him for an Urk. Everything about him, from his flat nose to his hairy feet, seemed too big. He walked in a hunched over, slouching way, almost as if he had no neck.

Iggy's skin prickled with sweat. *Noneck!* he thought, and his dad's words suddenly came back to him. 'If you meet a Noneck, run.' Right now this sounded like pretty good advice, except the Noneck was closing on them fast and carrying a spear. Running away would only make them look frightened – which obviously they weren't.

A few paces away the stranger halted and stared at them in silence. Iggy noticed the string of dirty yellow bones hanging at his chest. He had bone bracelets and anklets that rattled like teeth when he moved. The point of his spear was stained with mud – or at least it might have been mud.

'Hello,' said Iggy, feeling someone ought to break the silence.

'*Gnnnhh.*' The Noneck made a sound in his throat like a dog growling. It was hard to tell if this meant 'Welcome' or 'Prepare to die'.

'WE . . . ARE . . . URKS,' said Iggy, speaking as if the Noneck was hard of hearing. 'URKS. FROM THE TRIBE OF URK.'

'Urrgs,' said the Noneck.

Hubba whispered in Iggy's ear: 'I don't think he speaks Urkish.'

The Noneck's eyes shifted from Iggy to Hubba and back. He stabbed the ground with his spear and suddenly gabbled a stream of words.

'*Clug!*' he grunted. '*Burra burra clug! Ney ney hoo cumma clug!*'

Iggy and Hubba looked at each other wide-eyed.

'*Clug!*' repeated the Noneck, jabbing a finger at them impatiently.

'Maybe he wants to know who we are,' said Iggy. He pointed to himself. 'ME IGGY. HE HUBBA. HUBBA, IGGY.'

'*Piggy*,' said the Noneck.

'No, no – Iggy.'

'*Piggy.*'

Iggy decided this wasn't getting them far. 'WHO . . . ARE . . . YOU?' he asked, pointing a finger at the Noneck. 'Yes. Who are you? Who?'

'Yoo-who!' said the Noneck.

'No. What is your name? Me Iggy. WHAT – IS – YOUR – NAME?'

'Krakkk.'

Hubba wiped his eye. 'Is that his name or were he spitting?'

'Krakkk,' repeated the Noneck. 'Krakkk, Krakkk.' He repeated it several times, apparently liking the sound of it. Finally he turned and

pointed his spear the way he'd come.

'*CLUG!*' he barked and strode off into the grey mist.

Iggy looked at Hubba. 'Maybe he wants us to follow.'

'Mmm,' said Hubba.

'It can't do any harm.'

'Not unless he's planning to eat us.'

Iggy glanced at the darkening sky; it was

growing colder. 'I think we have to trust him,' he said. 'Maybe he knows where we can find some food.'

That settled it. They set off across the marsh, running to catch up with their guide.

Krakkk had a fire burning. Even better, he had two silver fish speared on sticks cooking over the flames. After days of living on nothing but roots, nuts and berries, the smell was heavenly. Iggy bit into the soft white flesh and was soon chatting about their journey and the valley they'd left behind. He knew Krakkk didn't understand a word, but their host nodded occasionally and made grunting noises. Nonecks weren't half as bad as his dad had made out, decided Iggy. Maybe Dad had never met one like Krakkk, who would share his last fish with you.

Iggy talked about Hammerhead's sickness and explained they were searching for a plant that could cure him of the fever.

'It's called the Purple Stankwort,' he said. 'Do you know it?'

Krakkk spat a fishbone into the fire.

'STANKWORT,' repeated Iggy. 'PURPLE STANKWORT.'

Krakkk pointed a finger at Hubba. 'Stinkwit,' he said.

'No,' said Iggy. 'It's a plant. A flower.'

'You know, like buttercups and daisies,' added Hubba.

'Doosies?' said Krakkk. He offered them the head of the last fish.

'This is hopeless. We're wasting us time,' said Hubba.

Iggy had an idea. If words were failing them, it might be easier to show their friend what they meant. He plucked a weed he found growing among the rocks.

'FLOWER,' he said, showing it to Krakkk. 'FLO-WER!'

Krakkk took it and put it in his mouth. '*Blumen*,' he said, chewing.

'Yes, *blumen*! We look for *blumen*. The *blumen* called Stankwort!' Iggy held his nose and pulled a face.

'Sorry,' said Hubba. 'Must have been all those nuts.'

A light of understanding dawned on Krakkk's face.

'*Reekblumen!*' he exclaimed.

'Yes, *Reekblumen!*' said Iggy excitedly. 'Where? Where is *Reekblumen*?'

'*CLUG!*' Krakkk jumped to his feet, grabbed his spear and waded off into the fog.

'Come on,' said Iggy.
'I think he knows.'

Chapter 7
Scent of the Stankwort

Ten minutes later they were standing at the edge of a bubbling brown bog where islands of marshweed poked their heads above the slime. Iggy clasped a hand over his mouth. Once when he was little he had stepped in a pile of mammoth dung and the smell had clung to him for days, but this was worse, much worse. It was like dead fish rotting in the sun. It seemed to be coming from a small patch of purple on one of the islands. Iggy's hopes rose. That had to be the Stankwort!

'Look,' he said, pointing. 'But how do we get to it?' He turned, but found to his surprise that he was addressing thin air. Hubba and Krakkk had disappeared. A minute ago they were all standing together, but now the other two had vanished without a word. Iggy guessed Hubba must have retreated to a safe distance where he could be sick. He covered his mouth with his furs, trying not to think too much about dying alone in a bog. They had come all this way to find the Purple Stankwort and he wasn't going to be put off by a bit of a stink.

*

He waded out into the bubbling bog and in no time had sunk up to his knees. This wasn't a good sign. Something slipped through the slime, leaving a trail of ripples in its wake. A shudder passed through Iggy. Were there such things as bog snakes, and if so how big were they? The mud oozed and slopped as he waded deeper, keeping

his eyes on the small patch of purple. A little further and he would be able to reach it. But his next step missed the bottom and warm mud rose up to his neck, slopping into his mouth. He was sinking deeper.

'HUBBA!' he cried. 'HEEEEELP!'

His muffled cry died away in the silence. Iggy closed his eyes. *Great*, he thought. *So this is where it ends: sinking in the world's smelliest bog.*

He thought of all the questions he would never be able to answer – like why you get fur in your belly button and why it never rains upwards. The Stankwort was so close his fingertips could almost touch it. He stretched out a hand, leaning forward and tasting another mouthful of slime. His fingers grazed the flower's stem. And then he felt it. Something cold slithering over his foot. It was starting to coil itself around his left leg.

ARGHHHHHHHHH!

Iggy took off as if his bottom was on fire.

The next thing he knew, he was lying on the bank, coated in sticky brown slime.

There was a disgusting smell in his nostrils. He looked down to find he was clutching a plant with a flower like a purple teardrop. The Stankwort. He almost wanted to weep with relief. Now all he had to do was find Hubba and they could finally go home. Everything was going to be OK. The Chief would get better and the black cloud hanging over him would be lifted. He stood up, dripping gobs of mud.

'Hubba! Where are you?' Slopping through the fog, Iggy tried to remember which direction they had come from.

'HUBBA?'

'Iggy! IGGY!'

The voice was a way off and somewhere to his left.

Iggy tucked the Stankwort inside his furs for safe keeping and broke into a run. He ducked under some trees and came to the clearing where they'd sat by the fire. Hubba was there. So was Krakkk, although now he didn't look quite as friendly. Maybe it was his wolfish smile – or the large army standing behind him. Like Krakkk, the other Nonecks were heavily built with short legs, flat noses and lumpy faces. They wore strings of bones and one of them was sporting an animal skull as a hat. They were armed with wicked-looking spears, which right now were pointing at Iggy's head.

'Sorry, Iggy,' sighed Hubba. 'I did try to warn you.'

'Oh? When was that?'

'When I shouted, "Iggy, Iggy!" I said it twice, see, which were code for: "I am took prisoner. Run!"'

'Thanks,' said Iggy. 'Obviously I should have guessed that.'

Krakkk stepped forward. He no longer looked like someone who would share his last fish with you. He smiled his twisted smile.

'So. We're meat again, Urk boy.'

Iggy stared in disbelief. 'You speak Urkish!'

'Not really,' muttered Hubba. 'His accent's terrible.'

'Yes,' said Krakkk, puffing out his chest. 'As matter of frogs, I speak many talks: Urkish, Vargish, Tiklish. Maybe you not believe? Maybe you think Krakkk is big stupids?'

'No!' protested Iggy.

'Yes. You Urks — always you think you are big

clevers. Plenty big caves. Plenty big hunters.'

'I wouldn't say that,' said Iggy. He tried to remember what he had talked about over supper. Obviously he should have been more careful, but he'd assumed Krakkk was too simple to understand. *If anyone's a big stupid*, he thought, *it's me. Dad tried to warn me about Nonecks but I thought I knew better.*

Krakkk was shouting something in his own

harsh language. He seemed to be the leader, because his men scuttled off quickly to obey. They were getting ready to move off.

'So,' said Krakkk, 'what way? You show Krakkk.'

'Show you?' said Iggy. 'Where are we going?'

Krakkk pushed his face so close that Iggy could smell his fishy breath. 'Velly of Urk,' he leered.

Chapter 8
Get Worse Soon

Back in the Valley of Urk, two figures were climbing the hill on the way to the Chief's cave. The older one was stocky and dark and strode ahead impatiently, carrying a sack tied at the neck. The younger trailed along behind sulkily.

'I thought you said he were dying,' grumbled Snark.

'He were,' replied Borg grimly. 'But now he's not.'

'Well, that's lucky, isn't it?'

'Lucky? *Lucky?*' Borg halted and stared at his son. 'Has you mud for brains? If he gets better then he'll still be Chief, won't he?'

Snark rubbed his nose. 'I thought *you* were gonna be Chief.'

'I were, but if that big blatherhead survives, then I won't, will I? That's why we has to make sure —' Borg broke off and glanced around, before lowering his voice — 'That's why we has to make sure he doesn't.'

'Doesn't what?'

'Doesn't live, you bonehead!'

Snark still looked confused. 'But I thought we was taking him a present.'

'So we are. Something he won't forget,' said Borg, with a nasty smile.

Snark glanced at the sack which his dad carried well away from his body. It looked empty, but he knew it wasn't because Borg refused to let him look inside or even go near it.

'Can I give it to him?' he asked.

'No!' snapped Borg. 'And remember, when we get there, what does you do?'

'Nothing,' said Snark.

'And what does you say?'

'Nothing.'

'Exactly. Let me do the talking and keep your blabber shut,' said Borg.

They had reached Hammerhead's cave. It was

easy to tell apart from the others because the entrance was framed by two great mammoth tusks forming an arch. A young, round-faced Urk called Orik stood guarding the entrance. He stood up straight when he saw them approach and gave the Urk salute, smiting himself twice on the forehead.

'How goes the Chief?' asked Borg. 'We come to pay us respects.'

Orik looked a little uncomfortable.

'Beggin' pardon, but my orders are no visitors.'

'Of course, of course,' said Borg. 'But I'm an elder – you can let me through.'

'All the same,' said Orik, 'orders is orders.'

Borg studied the sky for a few moments. 'Your name is Orik, isn't it?' he asked.

'That's right, Orik.'

'You like games, Orik?'

Orik's face brightened. 'Oh yes, I do love a game.'

'Then here's one for you. You try counting to ten, and if you can you win a prize.'

'Oh,' said Orik. 'I never played that one before. I got to count to ten?'

'That's it.'

Orik screwed up his face in concentration and began very slowly. 'One, two . . . um, two.'

'Tell you what, we'll make it five,' said Borg generously.

'Five, all right. One, two . . . um . . .'

'Three, four, five,' said Borg.

'That's it – three, four, five. I done it!' cried Orik excitedly. 'Does I win the prize?'

'Yes, you can go off duty.'

'Oh. You sure? But who'll be guarding the Chief?'

'We'll see to that, don't worry. Off you go now.'

Orik headed off down the hill, looking back to give them a cheery wave.

Borg waved back. 'Dungwit,' he muttered as they entered the cave.

*

Hammerhead was asleep in a corner on a thick bed of furs. A stale odour of woodsmoke and bat droppings filled the cave. Over the last few days the Chief had been battling the poison in his body. Sometimes he slept and sometimes he called out in his sleep. Sometimes he had strange dreams. He dreamed he was a boy again in short furs, then he dreamed he was a bunch of grapes, then he woke up and found he was biting his hand. Right now he was dreaming there were people in his cave and their ugly faces were staring down at him.

'Phwoar! His breath is proper rank!' said Snark, wrinkling his nose in disgust.

'Look at him,' sneered Borg. 'High Chief of the Urks. Not so high and mighty now, is he?'

It was true Hammerhead wasn't looking his best. His face was bathed in sweat. His wild red hair was matted and greasy and there were flecks of dribble in his beard. He rolled his head and moaned something that sounded like 'Wooor.'

'He wants some "wooor",' said Snark.

'Water, you fool.'

'Oh,' said Snark. 'Shall us fetch some?'

Borg smiled unpleasantly. 'No, we'll do better than that. Why don't we give him his present?'

He picked up the sack and carefully set it down close to the Chief's feet. Loosening the neck, he stepped back quickly. After a few seconds the sack began to twitch with life.

'What is it?' whispered Snark.

'I thought the Chief might like a bit of company. Come on, Snark, time us were going.'

They backed away and crept out of the cave, Borg dragging his son by the arm.

Hammerhead's eyes blinked open. With an effort he propped himself up on one elbow. A moment ago he was sure he'd heard voices, but now the cave was empty and silent – apart from a faint sound like the rustling of dry leaves. He looked down at his feet, where the noise seemed to be coming from. *Odd*, he thought. His feet had never made noises before.

A brown sack lay open on the ground and something was burrowing its way out. Something black and shiny. It had eight legs, a long, curved tail and tiny eyes like a scorpion's. Come to think of it, it was a scorpion! The tail arched over its back, quivering with its venomous sting. If this is a dream, thought Hammerhead, now would be a good time to wake up. He tried to cry out but his tongue felt like leather.

The scorpion tickled as it crept slowly up his leg. He wanted to laugh or scream or shake it off, but he knew any sudden move would be fatal. Sweat dripped down his pink face and lodged in the forest of his beard. The scorpion had reached his thigh and was climbing higher, scaling the mound of his belly. Hammerhead held his breath and kept very, very still.

Don't panic, he thought. *You've been in tighter spots than this . . .*

Chapter 9
Hubba Tries to Think of a Plan

Iggy picked his way over the stony ground. He'd never felt so weary. The Nonecks marched like an army in a hurry. They seemed to be able to cover miles at a time without talking, eating or stopping to admire the view. Every now and then Krakkk would halt and point his spear to the north or west, saying '*Onga?*' which seemed to mean 'Which way?'

Iggy had no idea which way – for all he knew they were hopelessly lost – but he thought it wiser not to mention this.

From what he could gather, the Nonecks were a nomadic tribe who moved from place to place. Right now they were looking for a winter home, and the Valley of Urk, they felt, would suit them perfectly. Krakkk had long been searching for the 'land beyond the river' that his grandfather had talked about. A place where the sky was always blue and berries grew on trees. It made no difference to him that the valley belonged to another tribe. If there was one thing the Nonecks loved, it was fighting battles.

*

Hubba drew alongside Iggy. 'Listen,' he said. 'Can you hear it?'

Iggy listened and heard a faint rumbling. It could be thunder, or it could be his stomach.

Over the rise of the hill they caught sight of it — the river. Iggy felt he'd never seen anything as beautiful in all his life. If this was the River Urk, then maybe they were getting close to home. Although it didn't look much like his own valley. Here the river rushed and swirled over rocks in a white torrent. The river that Iggy knew barely wibbled. One thing was certain: they would need to find a safer place to cross.

Krakkk was barking orders to his men. 'We rest now,' he told Iggy. 'Eat. Sleep. Tomorrow you take us Velly of Urk.'

Iggy said nothing. He longed to be home, but he wasn't keen to arrive with an army of Nonecks in tow. He needed to think of something – a plan, for instance. Krakkk had sat down against a log to watch his men set up camp. Iggy went over to join him.

'Don't you miss home?' he asked.

'Home?'

'The marshes.'

Krakkk wrinkled his nose. 'Marsh no good. Mud. Cold. Fog. Fish.'

'Fish?' said Iggy.

'Always fish. Fish for breakfast, fish for lunch, fish for slipper.' He spat on the grass in disgust.

'Velly of Urk much better. Better place for Nonecks.'

'It might not be,' said Iggy.

'Yes. You tell Krakkk. Nice big caves to sleep. Plenty hunt, plenty good meat.'

'Listen, about that . . .' said Iggy. 'I may have told a few fibs.'

Krakkk's face darkened. 'What is flibs?'

'You know – made it up, told some lies.'

Iggy didn't see where the axe came from, but he felt its blade pressed against his throat. 'You make flibs, Krakkk cut out your tongue. Good?'

Iggy nodded. 'Good,' he croaked.

Krakkk released him and went over to inspect the fire his men were building.

'That went well then?' said Hubba, flopping down on the grass.

Iggy rested his chin on his arms. 'Sorry. This is all my fault,' he sighed.

'What is?'

'Everything. Coming to the Farlands, getting captured, everything! And look where it's got us. We're leading an army back home so they can wipe out our whole tribe.'

Hubba patted him on the arm. 'You'll think of something.'

Iggy squinted at the sun glinting on the river far below. 'We have to warn them,' he said. 'We have to escape, find our way home and warn them.'

'See? I said you'd think of something,' Hubba grinned.

'Yes, but how? How can we escape when they're watching us all the time?'

Hubba chewed on a stalk of grass, thinking. 'We could always disguise ourselves?'

'As what?'

'Spiders,' said Hubba. 'That'd be best, see, cos they're probably scared of spiders.'

'Mmm,' said Iggy. 'I don't think that's going to work.'

Hubba shrugged and went back to thinking. 'All right, how's this?' he said. 'We lie low and wait for a storm. A proper big one.'

'And then?'

'Then they all get struck by lightning.'

Iggy thought that if Hubba came up with many more ideas, he might have to throttle him. The log they were sitting against shifted as he leaned back. Taking a closer look, Iggy saw it was hollow inside and crawling with centipedes. Yet the bottom half seemed solid enough.

'Hubba,' said Iggy, 'you remember that scootboard we made?'

'Yes.'

'Maybe we can do better.'

The sun had sunk behind the trees. Iggy glanced over at the Nonecks gathered round their fire. A hunting party had returned with a young deer, which was now roasting on a spit. Iggy noticed that their guards had been edging closer to the fire, anxious not to miss their share of supper.

'Right,' he whispered. 'When I say, "Now!" jump on.'

Hubba nodded.

Just then there was a howl of dismay as the meat fell off the spit and into the hot flames. The Nonecks leapt around, all shouting at once and trying to rescue their supper without burning their fingers. The guards had turned their backs. It was now or never.

'Go!' cried Iggy.

Hubba looked at him. 'You mean, go now?'

'Yes, NOW! Do it!'

Hubba jumped on the front of the log while Iggy pushed off from behind. It started to bump down the steep grassy slope as he jumped on. Suddenly they were hurtling downhill like a two-man toboggan. Iggy hung on for dear life. It was faster than the stone scootboard, maybe because the grass was wet and the hill alarmingly steep. The log hit a bump and for a few seconds they were airborne, landing with a thud that almost split the log in two. Behind, Iggy could hear the angry shouts of the Nonecks, who had just noticed their prisoners were escaping. He glanced over his shoulder and saw them racing down the hill. One of them lost his footing and went tumbling head over heels. A spear hummed through

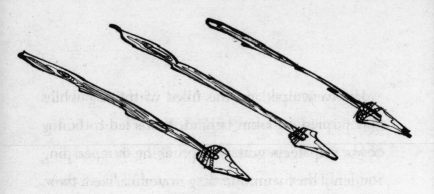

the air and Iggy ducked as it buried itself in the ground. Next moment the sky was raining spears. But Iggy didn't look back; he was staring over Hubba's shoulder at what lay ahead. They were hurtling towards the foaming white torrent of the river.

'Hold on!' he cried. 'We're going to . . .'

'YEEEARGHHHHHHHH!'

The log took off like a flying turnip and hit the river at roughly sixty-seven and a half miles an hour. There was a deafening splash. Then the world went dark and was filled with tiny bubbles and surprised-looking fish. Seconds later, the log bobbed up again with them clinging to it, gasping for air. The foaming white water carried them downstream, round the bend and out of sight.

*

Back on the riverbank, Krakkk raised his spear and with a howl of rage broke it over the head of the nearest soldier. 'STRUGA!'

His men looked shocked. That was a very rude word.

Chapter 10
A Heroes' Welcome

Iggy woke up. Something felt different. The birds were singing, the river was babbling quietly and Umily the Chief's daughter was stroking his hair. *Hold on*, he thought, *the last time I looked, Umily wasn't on the log at all. And another thing, the log is no longer rocking and lurching as if it might capsize at any moment.* He opened his eyes and blinked in the bright sunlight. The soft hand stroking his hair was a willow tree trailing its branches in the river. Evidently the log must have got tangled in it the previous night.

'Hubba?' said Iggy. 'Hubba! Wake up!'

'Uhhh?' Hubba raised his head. He stood up quickly, forgetting that he was on a floating log, and promptly overbalanced with a splash. He bobbed up, gasping for air and wearing a crown of green weed.

Once they had made it to the bank they looked around. It all looked strangely familiar.

'This is just like the Valley of Urk,' said Iggy.

'And them woods are like the Forest of Urk,' said Hubba, pointing.

'And look up there — aren't those our caves?

Hubba, you know what this means?'

'Somewhere else looks just like our valley?'

'No, we're home! The river has carried us home!'

The two of them whooped and hugged and danced for joy. Then Hubba pushed Iggy in the river just because he wasn't very wet, and they both splashed water over each other. Finally they remembered that they had urgent business and climbed the hill to the caves above. Iggy couldn't wait to see his mum and dad, to tell them of his adventures.

'Wait till they see us, he said. 'We'll probably get a heroes' welcome.'

*

Further up the hill, Dad had just managed to get a fire going. Mum emerged from the cave and rubbed her face wearily. They crouched beside the flames for a while, warming themselves in the cool morning air.

'I keep thinking maybe he'll turn up,' said Mum mournfully.

Dad shook his head. 'For Urk's sake! It's been days. You has to try and forget.'

'Poor little scroggler,' sighed Mum. 'I miss him.'

'I miss him too,' said Dad. 'I even miss all them dung-fool questions he used to ask.'

'And the things he were always bringing back – shells and feathers and scrubby old bones.' A tear rolled down Mum's cheek and plopped in the dust. 'Sometimes I imagine I can hear his voice.'

'MUM! DAD!' shouted Iggy from the bottom of the hill.

'Yes, like that, clear as mud,' said Dad.

'Hello? MU-UM!'

Dad stared. 'You would almost swear that were him.'

Mum stood up and clutched at her heart. 'Maybe it's his spirit come back,' she gasped.

'WHERE IS EVERYONE?'

'Look!' cried Mum. 'There, coming up the hill. It's him!'

'For a spirit, he's proper wet,' said Dad. 'And look, he's with the spirit of Hubba!'

Iggy reached the cave and stood before them, pale and out of breath.

Mum reached out a hand in wonder. 'Speak, Spirit,' she breathed. 'What is your message?'

'It's me, Mum. Iggy.'

'Iggy? My Iggy? Alive?'

'Yes!'

Mum touched his face and hair to convince herself he was real. Then she swung a hand and clouted him on the ear. 'Where has you been, you little scallybag? We thought you was dead!'

'OWW!' cried Iggy, rubbing his ear. 'It wasn't my fault! We got lost! And then we ran into Nonecks . . . but there isn't time to explain now. We need to see the Chief!'

'The Chief?' Dad shook his head. 'I'm afraid you're come too late.'

'What do you mean?' said Iggy.

'He were took bad last night. They say he can't last much longer.'

Iggy and Hubba hurried up the hill. As they drew near to the Chief's cave their ears were invaded by a terrible noise as if a hundred alley cats were practising the violin. A gaggle of ancient women with dirty faces and grey hair to their waists had

gathered outside. Iggy recognised them as the Wailing Widows. Whenever someone in the tribe died the widows hurried to the cave to weep and mourn outside. In Hammerhead's case they had obviously come early. There were five of them, wizened old witches who clawed at their furs and heaped dust and dirt on their heads.

'Woe! Woe!' they wailed. 'Woe to this day of sorrow!'

'Sorry,' said Iggy, trying to squeeze past, 'I can see you're busy, but could we see the Chief?'

One of the old crones gripped him by the wrist and fixed him with a glassy stare.

'Woe to the tribe of Urk!' she cried. 'Woe to the sons and the sons of sons – and the second cousins of the sons of sons . . .'

'This is urgent,' pleaded Iggy. 'If we don't see the Chief now, it might be too late.'

'For a day is coming,' crooned the mad-eyed witch, 'when tribe will rise against tribe, and foe against foe. Then woe to the tribe of Urk, for they are lost. LOST!'

'Woe and thrice woe and woe again for luck!' chorused the Widows.

Withered hands pawed at Iggy's face and arms. He would have been trapped there for some time if Hubba hadn't grabbed his arm and yanked him inside the cave.

'Thanks,' he panted. 'That was turning ugly. Where's the Chief?'

Hammerhead was lying on his soft bed of furs. He looked like Death, only with dirtier hair. His massive chest rose and fell with his raspy breathing. Around him were heaped burial offerings brought by the Urks: flintheads, axes and bits of carved bone. There were piles of hazelnuts and berries in case the Chief got peckish in the afterlife. The cave was sour with the smell of sickness. Iggy stared. He'd always imagined his uncle was invincible, as solid as the Standing

Stone, but now he looked frail and old.

Hubba bent down to pick something off the floor. It was the body of large black scorpion, minus its head. It seemed an odd gift to bring a dying Chief.

Hammerhead stirred and groaned, his cracked lips moving.

Iggy bent closer. 'It's Iggy, Uncle Ham. You

remember? We brought you something.'

He reached inside his furs and brought out the Purple Stankwort. It had got rather squashed and drooped limp as an old sock.

'That's her?' asked Hubba, who had never actually seen the plant. 'We went all the way to the Farlands for that soggy old bogweed?'

'Gaga said it was powerful magic,' said Iggy.

'Powerful smelly, if you ask me,' replied Hubba. 'How is he meant to eat her then?'

Iggy realised he hadn't given this any thought. Hammerhead looked too weak to chew anything. When he brought the Stankwort near his lips the Chief jerked his head away as if it was going to bite him.

'That's some stink,' marvelled Hubba. 'He can smell her with his eyes closed.'

Iggy heard raised voices outside the cave. They would have to act quickly. He found a shell full of rainwater and crushed the petals of the Stankwort into it. Propping his uncle's head up, he trickled the liquid into his mouth a little at a time. Much of it dribbled into his beard, but some went down. Hammerhead spluttered and began to cough.

Iggy waited for the plant to work its healing magic. Nothing happened. The Chief's eyes remained closed and his raspy breathing rose and fell.

'Maybe we should leave him to rest,' said Iggy.

*

Outside the cave, a small crowd had gathered with Borg and Snark at the front. Borg was flanked by two large Urks armed with spears. It didn't look like a welcome party.

'So it's true. You're back,' sneered Snark. He was wearing his wolf's-fang necklace, to show he was now a Son of Urk.

'Who said you could enter that cave?' demanded Borg.

'No one,' replied Iggy. 'We needed to see the Chief.'

Borg laughed dryly. 'The *old* Chief, you mean. Or perhaps you hasn't heard? A few things has changed since you was away.'

Borg was playing with a string of whalebones round his neck. Iggy suddenly remembered where he'd last seen them — Hammerhead had worn them at the Feast of Urks.

'You?' he said. '*You're* the new Chief?'

Borg spread his hands modestly. 'The elders felt it were for the best.'

'But you can't . . . not while Hammerhead is still alive!'

'Sadly not for much longer. A great pity.'

'Hur hur! A great pity!' laughed Snark.

'You planned this right from the start,' said Iggy, clenching his fists.

Borg's eyes flashed dangerously. 'Careful, little cub.'

'Everyone knows you wanted Hammerhead out of the way so you could take over!'

'Maybe you forget, you're speaking to your Chief.'

'You'll never be *my* Chief!' cried Iggy.

Borg glared at him icily for a few seconds, then turned to his guards.

'Orik, take these traitors to the snake pit.'

'Yeah, Orik, to the snake pit.' Snark grinned.

Iggy felt strong arms imprisoning him. 'Wait!' he said, struggling to escape. 'You can't do this!'

'That's the thing when you're Chief,' drawled Borg. 'You can do whatever you like.'

'Listen!' cried Iggy as they were dragged away. 'We came to warn you! You're all in danger!'

Borg sighed heavily and raised a hand to bring them back. 'What danger?' he said.

'They're coming,' said Iggy. 'The Nonecks are coming!'

The colour drained from Borg's face.

'Woe! Woe to the tribe of Urk!' cried the Wailing Widows, seizing the moment.

'SILENCE, you old crones!' thundered Borg. 'What nonsense is this? What Nonecks?'

'They took us prisoner, but we managed to escape,' said Iggy, talking fast. 'But they won't give up. They're looking for the Valley.'

'Impossible,' said Borg. 'You're making it up.'

'We seen them!' said Hubba.

'Then where are they now?'

'North of the river, on their way here,' replied Iggy.

'WOE!' wailed the Widows, falling on their knees. 'For tribe shall rise against tribe –'

'WILL YOU PUT A ROCK IN IT?' roared Borg.

Iggy explained what he knew. If Krakkk had any sense he would follow the river south, which would eventually lead him to the valley and the Urks' settlement. It was only a matter of time.

By now the crowd had been swollen by men and women coming out of their caves. The words 'Noneck', 'army' and 'what did he say?' were passed from one person to another. Panic was spreading like marmalade. Borg climbed on to a large boulder so he could be heard — and also because it made him look taller.

'Men of Urk!' he shouted, adding, 'And women,' just in time. 'You all know me. I am Borg, son of Yorg, your new Chief!'

Nobody cheered.

'There's no need to panic!' Borg went on. 'Believe me, there's no army and no invasion. Never since the time of our fathers has Nonecks come this far south . . .'

'Chief! Chief!'

Borg was interrupted by a young Urk barging his way through the crowd.

'They're coming!' he gasped. 'The Nonecks are coming!'

'WOE!' wailed one of the Widows. 'For the day of doom is —'

She was cut off by a large clod of mud landing a direct hit.

Chapter 11
Run for Your Lives!

Truth to tell, it had been many years since the Urks had fought a real battle. The last was the Battle of Urk Bottom (10067 BC), which was a famous victory over the Mumsi Tribe, though only the elders could remember it. At times like this the tribe needed a leader who was bold, fearless, and an axe-wielding maniac. Sadly Hammerhead was not available and they had to make do with Borg.

'What shall us do? Tell us!' they begged.

'Do?' said Borg, glancing anxiously back down the valley.

'You're our Chief. Lead us into battle!'

'Are you out of your tiny minds?' replied Borg. 'They are Nonecks! Savages! I could get killed!'

'But, Chief, what are us orders?' asked Orik.

'Do what you like,' snapped Borg. 'I'm going while there's still time.'

As he pushed his way through the crowd, the Urks dissolved in panic.

'FLEE!' they cried. 'Flee to the hills! Flee to the forest! Flee to the flee-side!'

In seconds everything was thrown into chaos.

People ran blindly to and fro, screaming and bumping into each other. Men hurried back to their caves to fetch whatever they could carry. Women scooped up crying infants in their arms and bellowed the names of children out playing on the hill. One of the elders woke up and wondered if the world was coming to an end. Amid all the confusion, somebody climbed on to a rock and yelled so loud that it stopped everyone in their tracks.

'WAIT!'

Iggy blinked, surprised to find he suddenly had the attention of the whole tribe. He realised he hadn't the faintest idea what he was going to say.

'What are you doing?' hissed Hubba. 'Get down!'

'Just back me up,' said Iggy. He cleared his throat. 'Listen,' he said. 'Why are you acting as if you're afraid?'

'We're not acting!' shouted an old man.

Iggy continued. 'This is our valley, our home. Are we just going to give it up without a fight?'

'What else can we do?' cried a woman, holding a baby. 'They are Nonecks! Giants!'

'They're not giants,' replied Iggy. 'I've seen them. They're not much bigger than me!'

Hubba was going to point out that this wasn't strictly true but thought better of it.

'We are Urks,' shouted Iggy. 'Never in our lives

have we run from anyone. Who will stand and fight? WHO IS WITH ME?'

His words were met by the sound of shuffling feet. Only Hubba's hand rose slowly in the air. Iggy caught sight of his dad trying to sneak away at the back.

'We're wasting us time,' said Orik. 'We can't fight them. We'd be cut to pieces!'

'Not if we're ready,' answered Iggy. 'Not if we work together.'

'How?' asked Orik.

Iggy took a deep breath. 'Listen. I've got an idea . . .'

That did it. People groaned and turned their backs. Iggy's shoulders drooped as he watched his audience melt away. He suddenly felt overcome with tiredness. After all, what did he know about fighting an invasion? He was only a boy.

WHUMP!

The ground shook like an earthquake. For a moment Iggy thought the Nonecks had arrived, then he turned to see the Standing Stone had toppled forward. There was only one man strong enough to have pushed it and he stood before them wild-eyed and pale as a ghost. Chief Hammerhead raised a finger and pointed at them accusingly. His voice rumbled like thunder.

'We are URKS! We fight like men! Listen to the boy!'

Having spoken these words, he swayed, putting out a hand to steady himself before collapsing like a tower of porridge.

Chapter 12
'What's That Coming Over the Hill?'

Iggy had been as astonished as anyone else at Hammerhead's sudden appearance.

In fact, what had happened was this: shortly after Iggy and Hubba had left the cave, the Chief had regained consciousness. The fever had left him weak and he felt like someone emerging from a long, deep sleep. Tottering to his feet,

Hammerhead had trodden on something on the floor. It was the body of a black scorpion which he dimly remembered killing with the axe he kept by his bed. A terrible stench of dead fish filled the cave and it made him want to get out before he threw up. Dragging himself down the hill, he had been surprised to see people running around like frightened ants and babbling about an invasion. That was the moment Hammerhead had felt dizzy and had leaned on the Standing Stone a little too heavily.

The Urks had no doubt it was a sign from the gods. The sacred stone had fallen and their Chief had appeared to them like someone back from the dead. He had spoken the words they must obey: 'Fight like men. Listen to the boy.'

As a result Iggy suddenly found he had a captive audience. The tribe hung on his every word, as if they believed he alone could save them. There was no time to be nervous or to wonder if his plan would work. He issued instructions and drew pictures in the dust. Soon men were cutting down branches and fetching bundles of furs from their caves. Women worked feverishly, threading the furs together to make what soon began to resemble a giant furry patchwork quilt.

Later that evening, as the shadows grew longer, the Nonecks swarmed across the river with their spears and axes held above their heads. Krakkk led the way, keeping his eyes fixed on the hills above for any sign of the enemy.

'*Menna husha*,' he said.

(It's quiet.)

'*Verra husha*,' came the reply.

(Too quiet if you ask me.)

They stole up the hill, silent as wolves in a library. But when they reached the Urk camp it looked deserted. Tools and flints lay abandoned on the ground, the fires were out and nothing stirred but the cold wind.

'*Clug!*' commanded Krakkk and a group hurried off to search the caves for anyone hiding. A few minutes later they were back, shaking their heads.

'*Scarpa*,' they grunted. Krakkk looked unconvinced. His eyes swept over the valley, watching the trees and rocks for any sign of movement. His instincts told him this was too easy. He spat on the ground, missed and wiped his foot on the grass.

Half a mile up the hill, the Urks waited in the woods, trying not to tremble too loudly.

'You're sure this'll work?' whispered Iggy's dad.

'Yes,' said Iggy. 'Hopefully.'

'*Hopefully?*'

'I've never tried it before,' said Iggy. 'Well, only on a snake.'

'Dung and blood!' groaned Dad, rolling his eyes. 'What do you call them things?'

'Clatterpults,' whispered Hubba. 'They're deadly!'

Iggy held up a hand for silence. He could hear voices.

The Nonecks were coming up the hill, just as he'd expected. Krakkk wouldn't be satisfied the Urks were gone till he had searched every inch of the valley.

Iggy peered out through the trees as the enemy came into view. He could hear their bone bracelets rattling like teeth.

'Now?' hissed Hubba.

Iggy shook his head. 'Wait for my signal.' He raised his hand high, then brought it swiftly down.

'What's the signal?' whispered Hubba.

'That *was* the signal!'

'Oh. You mean now?'

'Yes! Now! Now!'

FTAAAANNNGGGGG!

The twang of fifty jawbone catapults firing at once was a sound the Nonecks had never encountered. They halted uncertainly and looked up. Something dark rose out of the trees and into the sky. It could have been a flock of crows, but it wasn't.

'*Argh! Oof! Struga!*' The next moment they yelped and ducked as fifty doughnut-sized rocks came pelting down on them. Most of the Nonecks dived to the ground or ran for cover. But no sooner had they got to their feet than they were hit by a second bombardment as painful as the first.

'*Ogga flogga! Scarpa!*'

(The sky is falling on us! Run!)

'*Ouch! Arrrgh!*'

The Nonecks turned and would have fled, if Krakkk hadn't driven them back, promising he would personally split them down the middle with his axe if they gave up. They came back reluctantly, nursing their bruises and watching the sky in case it fell on them once again. Like most tribes, the Nonecks believed in magic, and they didn't like the look of this magic one bit.

*

Krakkk had spotted that the attack had come from the woods. He pointed his spear forward, ordering his men up the hill.

'*Onga!*'

They didn't get far. From somewhere in the trees came a noise that struck terror into their hearts: a long drawn-out snarl like the roar of some savage beast. The advance faltered, threatening to become a retreat. Even Krakkk looked shaken as the ground trembled. A moment later they saw it rise over the crest of the hill: a brown shaggy monster as big as a house.

'*WAMMOTH!*' cried the Nonecks.

They had seen mammoths before, but never one as ugly and misshapen as this. One tusk pointed upwards while the other seemed to be signalling left. It came over the hill wobbling and shaking, its shaggy coat flapping like a tent.

The Nonecks backed down the hill. The beast

had reached the top of the slope and was gathering itself to charge. A charging mammoth can reach a top speed of fifty miles an hour — but no one seemed to have told this one. It thundered down the hill like a runaway caravan, bumping and rocking and shedding lumps of fur.

'*Struga!*' yelled Krakkk, hurling his spear.

'*Scarpa!*' screamed the Nonecks, dropping their weapons and scattering in terror.

'ATTACK!' roared Chief Hammerhead, as the Urks burst from the trees, waving their axes and uttering their famous war cry.

Ugga ugga oogie!
Urk! Urk! Urk!

In less than ten minutes the Battle of Urk Woods (10002 BC) was over. The Nonecks fled down the slope, plunged across the river and were last seen disappearing into the forest.

Chapter 13
Iggy, Son of Urk

If Krakkk had looked back he might have been surprised to see the giant mammoth had given up the chase. It had picked up speed, racing towards the river before ploughing straight into a pine tree. One of its tusks fell off and it toppled sideways, landing with a heavy thud.

When the dust had settled Iggy crawled out from the wreckage and sat down with a groan.

Moments later Hubba and several more of the Sons of Urk spilled out looking pale and dazed. Bits of the 'mammoth' lay scattered over the hill, for in reality it was made of little more than bones, furs and a lot of imagination.

Iggy looked about him at the deserted battle-field. 'What happened?'

'We won!' said Hubba. 'They ran away!'

'You see? I told you it would work!'

Hubba felt a lump on his head. 'Yes,' he said. 'But next time I'm doing the steering.'

Iggy examined one of the scootboards that had launched them down the hill. The front was slightly dented.

'Perhaps it needs something else?' he said.

'Something to make it stop.'

Loud voices announced Hammerhead and his victorious army had returned from the river. For most of the battle the Chief had led his troops from a lying-down position in the shade of a tree. Only once it became clear that the enemy was running away had he felt well enough to lead the attack.

Iggy was surprised to see Umily among the Urk warriors, muddy-faced and armed with a bone catapult. He was even more surprised when she caught his eye and smiled at him. He grinned back, remembering just in time to close his mouth so he didn't look like a gormless Urk.

*

'Well,' said Hammerhead, 'they won't be back in a hurry. Has you seen 'em running from me?'

The Urks looked at each other, wondering who ought to tell him.

Iggy's dad cleared his throat. 'Er, Hammy? I think they were running from the mammoth.'

'No! You mean they thought it were real?'

'That were the idea.'

'By the horn of Urk! Where's Iggy? It's him we should be thanking.'

Iggy came forward a little sheepishly, clutching the dented scootboard. He was worried his uncle might still blame him for the accident with the snake. But Hammerhead was speaking to Dad and

when he turned back he had something in his hand.

'I think this belongs to you, young Iggy,' he said, holding it out.

Iggy stared. It was a wolf's-tooth necklace.

'To me?'

'Certainly, if you're going to be a Son of Urk.'

Iggy bowed and Chief Hammerhead slipped the necklace over his head. Hubba was the first one to cheer and the rest of the tribe joined in, chanting, 'Urk! Urk! Urk!' and jabbing their spears in the air. Iggy stood in the middle of them with his eyes shining and a smile as wide as the river. At long last he was a warrior like his father and his grandfather before him. It had turned out to be a lot harder than killing a grass snake, but he'd got there in the end.

'Now, my boy,' said the Chief, putting a large arm round him. 'This idea of yours, what does you call her?'

'Oh. A scootboard,' said Iggy.

'Scootboard, hmm? And how's her work exactly?'

Iggy did his best to explain. He showed the

Chief how he'd improved the design by adding wooden rollers at the front and back, to increase the speed and iron out the bumps.

'And anyone can do it?' asked Hammerhead.

Iggy nodded. 'Anyone.'

'It's deadly!' enthused Hubba. 'It feels like you're flying.'

'Flying, eh?' Hammerhead's eyes lit up. He had always wondered what it would feel like to fly.

*

Ten minutes later a big crowd gathered at the top of the hill to see the first ever attempt by an Urk Chief to ride a scootboard.

'You sure this is a good idea?' whispered Dad. 'This morning he were still on his deathbed.'

'As long as he avoids the trees he'll be fine,' said Iggy.

Hammerhead was looking down the hill a little nervously. It looked a lot steeper than he remembered. 'Right. So I just push off, does I?'

'Yes, push off and let her go,' said Iggy.

Hammerhead took a deep breath. He placed one foot on the scootboard, mouthed a prayer to the gods and pushed off hard. The scootboard leapt

forward. It trundled at first, then gained more and more speed as it dipped down the slope. Hammerhead wobbled and swayed, his face red, his arms paddling the air as he tried to stay on.

At the top of the hill the Urks whooped and cheered, urging their leader on.

'Go, Chief! Go, Chief!'

'He missed the trees!'

'Look at him go!'

'He's flying!'

'He's heading for the river!'

'How's he going to . . .'

SPLASH!

. . . stop?'

Iggy coughed. 'Obviously I'm still working on that.'

The End

Chapter 14
One More Thing

Meanwhile, high in the hills, two Urks were huddled in a cave, hiding from the Noneck invasion.

'You think we're safe?' asked Snark.

'Course we're safe,' snapped Borg.

'But what if they follow us tracks?'

'They won't. Long as we stay here and doesn't make a sound, they'll never find us.'

Snark pressed his cheek against the cold rock, trying not to make a sound. It was dark in the cave, much darker than their cave in the valley. He couldn't see his hand in front of his face, though maybe that was because he was sitting on his hands.

'Stop sniffing!' said Borg.

'I'm not. It smells!'

'Caves always smell.'

'This one smells funny,' whined Snark.

He sniffed the air. It was a smell he didn't recognise. Strong and earthy. For some reason it made the hairs rise on the back of his neck.

'Can't you stop snuffling?' grumbled his dad.

'I told you, I'm not!'

'You are! You been doing it since we got here.'

'That's you,' said Snark.

'It's not me!'

'Then who is it?'

They fell quiet and listened. Snark could hear it plainly now. Slow, snuffly breathing. It echoed in the cave. Snark reached out a hand but felt nothing except the cold, clammy wall. Getting up, he shuffled deeper into the cave, feeling his way with his hands out in front of him. His fingers brushed something silky soft like fur. Fur that was warm and alive and furry. He blinked. In the dark, two large brown eyes were staring back at him.

'Dad!' he hissed urgently, backing away.

'What now?'

'There's a b-b-bear in here!'

'Don't be a dungwit!'

'There is!'

They heard an angry grunt and the bear lolloped towards them on all fours, huge and dark and rolling her great furry head.

'GRRRRRRRRRRRRRRRRRRR!' she growled.

'Snark,' gasped Borg.

'Yes?'

'When I count to three, run like the wind.'

Snark nodded, speechless with terror.

'Three!'

They ran – back through the cave, out into the light and scrambling down the hill without pausing to look back.

The bear lumbered back into her cave and sat

down. She sniffed the air.

Cheek! she thought. *I can't smell anything at all.*

Look out for the next exciting adventure starring
Iggy the Urk

Coming from Bloomsbury in
September 2010

Also by Alan MacDonald

HISTORY *of* WARTS

Custardly Wart
Pirate (Third Class)
ALAN MacDONALD

Ditherus Wart
(Accidental) Gladiator
ALAN MacDONALD

Honesty Wart
Witch Hunter!
ALAN MacDONALD

Sir Bigwart
Knight of the Wonky Table
ALAN MacDONALD